For the lovely Ina

Text for this book was hand lettered by Ross Collins

Published by Bloomsbury, New York and London
Distributed to the trade by St. Martin's Press
Library of Congress Cataloging-in-Publication Data
Collins, Ross. Busy night / Ross Collins. p. cm.  Summary: After Ben goes to bed,
the Tooth Fairy, the Sandman, Santa Claus, and others come into his room and argue
so loudly that they wake him up. [1. Sleep—Fiction.  2. Characters in literature—Fiction.]
1. Title: PZ7.C6836 Bu 2002    [E] dc-21  2001043863

ISBN 1-58234-750-6
First U.S. Edition
Printed in Hong Kong
1 3 5 7 9 10 8 6 4 2

Bloomsbury USA Children's Books
175 Fifth Avenue
New York, New York 10010

# Busy Night

## Ross Collins

BLOOMSBURY
CHILDREN'S
BOOKS

"Just five more minutes," yawned Ben.
"Pleeaase ..."

"Look at you," said Ben's mother.
"Barely enough energy to play with
your loose tooth.
Get off to bed - pronto."

Ben crawled upstairs to bed.

Ben washed his face,

brushed his teeth,

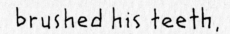

put on the bunny pajamas
which nobody knew about,
and got under the covers.

**CLICK!** Out went the light, and so did Ben. The clock in the hall struck nine and all was quiet.

Except,

**CRREEAAAK**, the window was opening ...

A strange little figure hauled his huge pockets into Ben's room.
He poked Ben's nose and began to softly sing.

"The Sandman's here, the Sandman's here,
Boys and girls have nothing to fear.
With a sprinkling of sand around your bed,
Good, sweet dreams will dance in your head.
Of peaches and cream and liquorice shoes,
Of lemonade navels and ... "

"OY!" interrupted a disgruntled voice.

"GET A MOVE ON, SANDY PANTS!"

It was the Tooth Fairy.
And she was late.

"SOME OF US HAVE
TEETH TO COLLECT,"
she said.

The Sandman
stopped sprinkling his sand.

"Quiet, you," he whispered,
"The Creature is only dozing
and I haven't finished my song yet."

"LOOK, SANDWICH," said the fairy,
"I'VE GOT A WHOLE GOBFUL OF MOLARS TO
GRAB BY MIDNIGHT AND YOU'RE HOLDING UP
THE SCHEDULE."

"Shhhhhh!" said the Sandman,
"We shouldn't wake the ..."

"WOOOOOOOOOOO!"
interrupted a new voice.

It was the Ghosts.

"WOOOO RATTLE RATTLE!"

There was a pause, then they said it again.
"WOOOO. RATTLE RATTLE."
"IT'S A-HAUNTIN' TIME." they wailed,
"RUN IN TERROR!"

"BUG OFF!" said the tooth Fairy.

"Pipe down, boys," said the Sandman.
"Maybe if we lined up..."
"I haven't even seen an incisor yet," said the tooth Fairy.
"WOOOO..." started the Ghosts, but they were interrupted
by a loud "THBBTHBPTHH!"

"WHAAT WAAS THAAATT?"
whispered the ghosts.
"It came from under the bed,"
gulped the Sandman.
"THBBTHBP! SLAP!
GURGLE! BLABTHH!"
went a gurgly voice.

"I AM THE THING~UNDER~THE~BED AND I COME
OUT ... JUST ABOUT NOW! BFHT!" gargled the voice.
"What do you look like?" asked the Tooth Fairy.
"WHATEVER GIVES YOU THE WILLIES," came the voice.
"TONIGHT I WILL BE GREENY PURPLE.
NOW GO AWAY!"

Everybody was a little scared
by the Thing-Under-the-Bed,
especially the Ghosts.
"NOOBODY TOLD US ABOUT
HIIMMMMMM," they said.
"Just one wisdom tooth
and I'm off," said the Tooth Fairy.
"THBTHPBT! RASP!"
said the Thing-Under-the-Bed.
"I'VE GOT TENTACLES! AND BIG..."
CRUUMMPF!
He was interrupted by a noise in the fireplace.

"HO! HO! HO!" said a booming voice.
It was Santa Claus.

Everybody looked at him, then at each other, then back at Santa.

"IT'S NOT EVEN CHRISTMAS!!" they all yelled together.

"ISN'T IT?" asked Santa.

"NOOo!!"

"Blast those elves!" said Santa. "Second time I've fallen for that this year."

Even the Thing-Under-the-Bed came out for a peek.

"LOOK, EVERYONE!" shouted the tooth Fairy.

"HE'S SOFT! GET HIM!"

Everybody jumped on the Thing-Out-from-Under-the-Bed and started arguing.

WHO WANTS A TOOTH LOOSENED?

WOOOOOO!

MUNCH!

OH NO!

BFFTHT!

KEEP THE NOISE DOWN CHAPS!

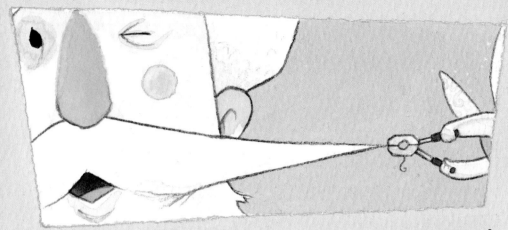

THIS ISN'T AT ALL CHRISTMASSY!

BLECH!

JUST ONE MOLAR!

WOOOMF!

I WAS HERE FIRST!

But then they were all interrupted. "AH-HEM!"

SOME OF US ARE TRYING TO GET SOME SLEEP AROUND HERE!

So they did.

"So what are we going to do now?"
"I hear Mary Cuthbertson across the street has a
loose tooth."
"RATTLE."

"Is it Christmas yet?"

"Does she like tentacles?"